# TELL ME A STORY,
# PAINT ME THE SUN

## When a Girl Feels Ignored by Her Father

# TELL ME A STORY, PAINT ME THE SUN

When a Girl Feels Ignored by Her Father

by ROBERTA CHAPLAN, Ph.D.

illustrated by Michael Chesworth

MAGINATION PRESS • NEW YORK

Library of Congress Cataloging-in-Publication Data
Chaplan, Roberta.
    Tell me a story, paint me the sun : when a girl feels ignored by
her father / by Roberta Chaplan ; illustrated by Michael Chesworth.
        p.    cm.
    Summary: When her father loses his job and withdraws from her
life, Sara feels confused and unworthy until her teacher helps her
to realize her own "specialness" despite a disappointing experience
with her dad.
    ISBN 0-945354-24-X (paper)
    [1. Fathers and daughters — Fiction.    2. Self-respect — Fiction.]
I. Chesworth, Michael, ill.    II. Title.
PZ7.C3656Te    1991
[Fic] — dc20                                                        91-7233
                                                                          CIP
                                                                          AC

Published by Magination Press, an Imprint of Brunner/Mazel, Inc.,
19 Union Square West, New York, NY 10003

Distributed in Canada by Book Center, 1140 Beaulac St.,
Montreal, Quebec H4R 1R8, Canada

Manufactured in the United States of America

10 9 8 7 6 5 4 3 2 1

# About this Book

Recent research has illuminated the powerful role of the father in a child's development. If the father-daughter bond is interrupted when the father turns away due to divorce, depression, work stress, or alcoholism, for example, the daughter is profoundly affected. Her sense of self-esteem suffers, as she generally blames herself for the loss. Addressing this issue at a young age is a step toward prevention of later difficulties.

*Tell Me a Story, Paint Me the Sun* describes the sadness and confusion of a girl whose father becomes depressed when he loses his job. Sara does not understand his withdrawal and begins to doubt herself and become angry at other people in her life. She then learns to understand, through the help of her teacher, that she is still special even though her father cannot respond to her.

Through reading about Sara's experiences, young people will realize that when a parent does not respond to them, it is not their fault, and that there are many other people who can love and appreciate them. They will learn that expressing their sadness is the first step to feeling whole. And most importantly, they will discover that whatever happens in their lives, they can look inside for their own strengths; they are not merely victims of circumstances.

# Chapter One

In summer, my dad and I would take walks together along the beach. We both wore brown leather sandals, the color of a dark penny. We liked to collect the different kinds of seashells sprinkled on the wet sand. Sometimes we dug out the closed sandy clams. Then we'd tap the edges to open them and see who was living inside.

Being with my dad made me feel strong and happy—like the sun was shining from inside my heart.

My dad worked in a big store that sold tools and building supplies. Every morning, my mom would cook breakfast for us all. Dad

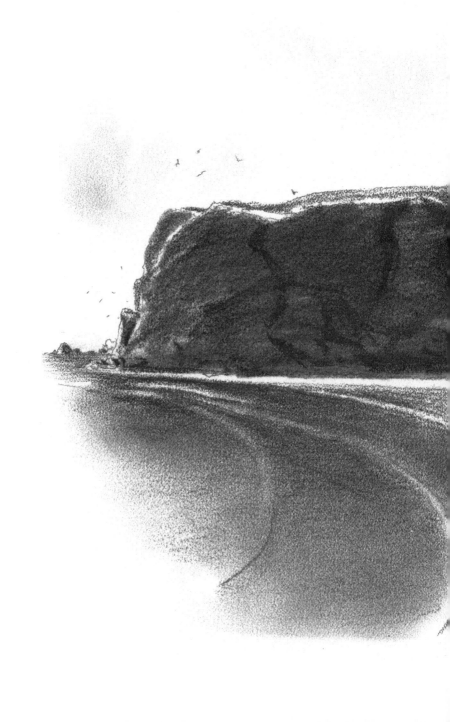

would eat real fast and rush off for work. Mom and I would clean up. Then she'd go to work and I'd go to school.

Some nights Dad came home late, after I was asleep. So, mostly I saw him on Sundays, his only day off. We'd usually go for a walk together. Then Dad would watch sports on television. I'd pop some popcorn and keep him company.

One night, when I was in bed, I heard Mom and Dad talking. It was real quiet in our house so I could hear most of what they said.

Every once in a while, there was a thud, like Dad was pounding his fist hard on our kitchen table. Then I heard choking sounds, a little like coughing, but more like crying.

"Get a grip on yourself, Paul," Mom said. "It's only a job."

"But you don't understand. I'll never find another job. I'm all washed up. I'm completely finished."

I couldn't sleep that night. Dad sounded so afraid. What if something really bad happens to him? What if he doesn't get another job? What if he doesn't come home anymore? I saw Dad cry once, when Grandma died, but this was different, and much scarier.

The next morning at breakfast, Dad was staring straight out the kitchen window. My stomach felt funny, like it was getting ready for a big stomachache. Nobody said anything, so I just ate real fast and went to school.

When I came back, I went straight to my room and called my friend Beth. We talked for two hours, mostly about our school play.

Dad was in the living room reading the newspaper when I came downstairs.

"Can you come to my play Thursday night?" I asked him, crossing my fingers. "Mom has to go to a meeting."

"Oh, Sara," he said, jerking his head up as if I had startled him. He looked at me

for a moment. Then he said, "I'll be sure to be there."

# Chapter Two

The day of our performance, we brought our costumes to school and had our last rehearsal before the play. I wore a yellow silk dress which came down to the floor and had long flowing sleeves. I played the part of a princess who had all the toys and clothes she wanted, but was still unhappy.

Beth played the role of the mean queen mother who loved her jewelry more than people. There were servants and cooks and magicians and hunters in the play. Everyone had a special part and a fabulous costume. Billy's was everyone's favorite. He was a magician and wore pointed silver shoes and

a blue velvet turban with a huge red ostrich feather.

The final rehearsal lasted for almost three hours because a lot of kids kept forgetting their lines. Everybody was nervous — except Ms. Chelsea. She kept telling us we were doing a great job.

No one went home for dinner. We all brought sandwiches and went to the cafeteria and sat together at one big table. Our stomachs were churning so much we could hardly eat.

Since this was my first play, I felt nervous, but very excited. As soon as I walked on stage, I knew that I would remember my lines.

I looked out at the faces in the audience hoping to find Dad, but he wasn't in the first three rows. I didn't know where he was sitting.

Soon the play was over, and the audience was applauding. The bright lights went on.

Maria's dad jumped on stage and snapped her picture. Then he gave her flowers and called her sweetheart. More parents came on stage, bringing flowers and taking pictures. Everyone was hugging.

I looked all around for Dad, but I couldn't find him anywhere. My friends and their parents started drifting down the grey aisles of the auditorium. My heart jumped each time the rear double door slammed shut. I kept hoping it would open again and Dad would be there smiling.

For a moment I thought I saw him waiting for me in the back of the auditorium, but it was just a gloomy shadow. The auditorium grew darker.

# Chapter Three

I felt like I was the only person on earth, when Ms. Chelsea came over to ask who was taking me home. I told her I was waiting for my dad.

"Do you want me to take you home?" she asked. "It's getting pretty late."

"Oh, that's alright," I said. "I'll just wait a little longer."

"Would you mind if I wait with you? It's no fun to be here alone."

Ms. Chelsea and I waited for another half hour. Then we decided to phone Dad and see if he was home. There was no answer.

"Why don't you come home with me?" Ms.

Chelsea asked. "We'll keep calling until someone answers."

Ms. Chelsea's house was warm and cozy. We both drank hot chocolate out of thick white mugs and ate oatmeal cookies. The next time Ms. Chelsea called, Mom answered the phone. She came right over.

Dad was home when we got back. I could see the top of his head resting on the soft velvet chair. Newspapers were scattered on the floor of the dark living room.

"What happened, Paul? Why weren't you at the play?"

Dad looked at the two of us kind of puzzled, as though he just woke up.

"Don't worry about it, Sara," Mom said to me. "He forgot. It's been a long day."

I felt really let down, but I didn't say anything. I went to bed and hid myself under the covers, pretending to be in my own private cave. I didn't even say goodnight to Mom. I felt too miserable.

# Chapter Four

Dad began to stay home all of the time, sleeping late, wearing his pajamas in the middle of the day.

He sat in a chair, his eyes staring off into space. I wanted to talk with him, but he seemed so far away. He hardly ever laughed, and he was very quiet. Sometimes he would walk quickly around the room, and then he'd sit down again. I felt that he didn't even know I was there.

When I suggested we go for a walk on Sunday, Dad said, "Okay," but he seemed so tired. He could barely move from his chair.

As we walked along together, neither of

us said very much. Dad looked a little like a sleepwalker who didn't know where he was. Whenever I said something to cheer him up, Dad didn't answer. Pretty soon I stopped talking.

I felt kind of embarrassed when our neighbors walked by and Dad didn't say hello to them. I guess he didn't notice. But I waved and said, "Hi." I wanted everything to be okay for Dad. So I walked with him in silence and tore leaves off the bushes, crumpling them in my hand.

When we got back Dad took a nap. Mom was in the kitchen cooking fried chicken.

"What's wrong with Dad?" I asked her. "He's acting so strange."

"Your dad is just tired," she said. "Go and set the table, Sara."

Mom was leaning over the stove, her hands full of batter.

# Chapter Five

One morning, as Beth and I walked to school together, I noticed Maria's dad dropping her off in his silver car with smooth red seats. He gave her a big hug and then touched her shining black hair. They smiled at each other.

"Why don't I have long pretty hair like Maria?" I thought. "I wish I could look like Maria, then I'd be special, too."

Maria was in front of me when we lined up to have our homework checked. As we moved down the line toward Ms. Chelsea's desk, I touched Maria's long hair to see what it would feel like. It was soft and silky, so I touched it again.

Maria swirled around. She had a mean look on her face. "If you don't stop pulling my hair, I'll scratch you," she hissed.

"You won't scratch me, you little rat," I growled. And I punched Maria on the back over and over, pounding with my fists.

Ms. Chelsea came to break up the fight, and I began to cry. I had never hit anybody so hard before. Ms. Chelsea made us go back to our seats, but she didn't punish me. "Are you okay?" was all she wanted to know.

"I'm sorry I hit her so hard. But I didn't really pull her hair. I just touched it."

Later that day, Ms. Chelsea said, "I was wondering if you would like to come over to my house this Saturday and paint a picture with me. It would be nice to have your company."

# Chapter Six

I couldn't wait until Saturday. I was so glad when Mom said I could go to Ms. Chelsea's house and she would drive me.

Even though it was raining pretty hard Saturday morning, I didn't mind. I was really excited as we drove to Ms. Chelsea's house. But then I began to feel a little scared.

Would anyone else be there? How would we spend the time together? Usually, I painted alone at home, and I never painted a picture for a whole day.

Mom kept talking about Aunt Harriet's new couch and how she wished she could buy new furniture for our living room.

As soon as we got to Ms. Chelsea's house, the red and pink flowers in her garden made me feel better. The rain had almost stopped, and my heart was thumping as we rang the doorbell. When Ms. Chelsea came to the door and smiled, I was certain everything would be alright.

As soon as Mom left, Ms. Chelsea showed me her art studio at the back of her house. We spread newspapers across a big white table and laid out our painting papers. Then we uncovered little pots of paint. There was one for each color.

"How's your father?" Ms. Chelsea asked in a soft voice while she stirred the yellow paint.

"Oh, he's fine," I said, feeling my stomach pinch from the inside.

"Did you ever find out why he didn't come to the play?"

"Oh, he just forgot."

# Chapter Seven

"Would you mind if I tell you a story?" Ms. Chelsea asked, smiling at me.

"When I was a young girl, just about your age, I lived in the country with my mother and father and sister. My father worked all the time, so we hardly ever saw him. When he was at home, he didn't pay much attention to us. It seemed that he was always thinking about something. He'd get a faraway look in his eyes, almost a sad look.

"When I think back now, I realize that my father hurt my feelings. I felt there was something wrong with me. I didn't like the way I looked. I thought my legs were too skinny. I was jealous of my friends who spent time with their fathers. I felt that I wasn't special like the other girls.

"Of course, I didn't know why I felt this way. And nobody else guessed how I felt — except my uncle Kenny. He must have noticed that I was being kind of quiet. Or maybe he read the sad expression on my face.

"Well, one Sunday, Uncle Kenny took me out for the day. We went to an amusement park, and he took me on all of the rides. We laughed at our fat and curvy and thin reflections in the house of mirrors. We let the man guess our weight, and he got us both right. We filled bottles with sand of different colors.

"While we were resting and eating cotton candy, Uncle Kenny said the nicest thing, as if he could read my mind.

"'You know, honey,' he said, 'you're a really special little girl. You are pretty and talented, too. Your daddy can't see these things about you because he has other things

on his mind. It's nice to have a daddy who can see your qualities shining like stars in the skies, but sometimes that doesn't happen. The truth is, you are still beautiful and special. You have many gifts to share with others. Next time you are sad remember how special you really are.'"

# Chapter Eight

Without really knowing it, while I was listening to Ms. Chelsea's story, I painted a big bright yellow sun. Around the outside of the sun, I painted tiny baby tears.

"You are as bright and beautiful as that sun," said Ms. Chelsea softly, "and your tears are beautiful, too. When you feel sad, imagine that the sun is crying. It is still bright and shining and beautiful and strong, but sometimes even the sun is sad."

Then Ms. Chelsea gave me a big warm hug. It felt so good to let out all of those stored up tears.

Since that day, I paint or draw pictures almost every day. Sometimes I write poems and stories. I know I have many gifts inside me, just like Ms. Chelsea, gifts I can share with others. And I know there are people in my life who can make me feel good, like the sun is shining from inside my heart.

Tomorrow I am going to Ms. Chelsea's house with some other kids from my class to paint sets for our next play. On Sunday, a new friend is coming over to spend the day. We're going to read our poems to each other. Next week, Beth and I are going on a bike trip.

When I get sad, sometimes I cry, but then I think about what Ms. Chelsea said, and I remember the bright yellow sun.

# MAGINATION PRESS BOOKS

**Julia, Mungo, and the Earthquake:** A Story for Young People About Epilepsy

**Tell Me A Story, Paint Me the Sun:** When A Girl Feels Ignored by Her Father

**Night Light:** A Story for Children Afraid of the Dark

**Putting on the Brakes:** Young People's Guide to Understanding ADHD

**The Potty Chronicles:** A Story to Help Children Adjust to Toilet Training

**Tanya and the Tobo Man:** A Story in English and Spanish for Children Entering Therapy

**Wish Upon A Star:** A Story for Children With a Parent Who Is Mentally Ill

**Gran-Gran's Best Trick:** A Story for Children Who Have Lost Someone They Love

**Scary Night Visitors:** A Story for Children with Bedtime Fears

**Ignatius Finds Help:** A Story About Psychotherapy for Children

**Jessica and the Wolf:** A Story for Children Who Have Bad Dreams

**The Blammo-Surprise! Book:** A Story to Help Children Overcome Fears

**Zachary's New Home:** A Story for Foster and Adopted Children

**Clouds and Clocks:** A Story for Children Who Soil

**Sammy the Elephant and Mr. Camel:** A Story to Help Children Overcome Bedwetting

**Otto Learns About His Medicine:** A Story About Medication for Hyperactive Children

**Double-Dip Feelings:** Stories to Help Children Understand Emotions

**This is Me and My Single Parent:** A Workbook for Children and Single Parents

**This is Me and My Two Families:** A Workbook for Children in Stepfamilies

**Cartoon Magic:** How to Help Children Discover Their Rainbows Within

**Robby Really Transforms:** A Story About Grown-Ups Helping Children

**Lizard Tales:** Observations About Life